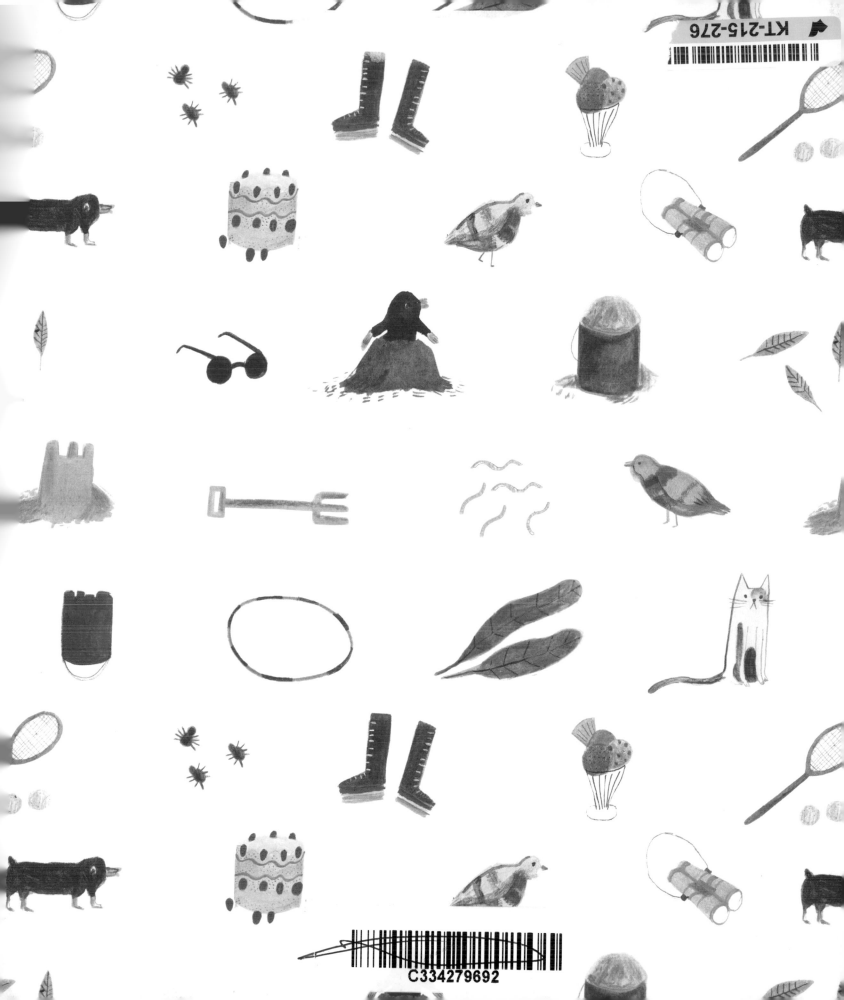

For Auntie B. and Auntie M., who always
wanted me to go and play with that
little boy over there.
C. B.

For Baby Noah, I hope your life is filled with
lots of adventures as exciting as this one!
M. P. S.

Translated from the French *Va Jouer Avec Le Petit Garçon!*

First published in the United Kingdom in 2018
by Thames & Hudson Ltd, 181A High Holborn,
London WC1V 7QX

www.thamesandhudson.com

First published in the United States of America
in 2018 by Thames & Hudson Inc., 500 Fifth Avenue,
New York, New York 10110

www.thamesandhudsonusa.com

Original edition © 2016 Éditions Sarbacane, Paris
This edition © 2018 Thames & Hudson Ltd, London

British Library Cataloguing-in-Publication Data.
A catalogue record for this book is available from
the British Library

Library of Congress Control Number 2018934204

ISBN 978-0-500-65170-4

Printed in France

HELLO, MONSTER!

Clémentine Beauvais & Maisie Paradise Shearring

Thames & Hudson

While I'm playing on my own in the park, Mum calls to me from her bench. I know what she's going to say.

"Go and play with that little boy over there! The one in the sandpit with the spade. He's all on his own. Go and say hello!"

I hate, hate, HATE saying hello
to little boys in sandpits.

After all, my mother wouldn't like it
if I did the same thing to her.

"Go and talk to that lady over there!
She must be bored, with only pigeons
to talk to. I bet she's really friendly!"

I can't imagine my mum saying hello
to people she doesn't know.

In fact, she often tells me not to talk to strangers.

Yet she's never seen that little boy before
and she wants me to go and play with him.
She thinks he's perfectly safe. But I'm not so sure.

What if that little boy isn't REALLY
a little boy at all?

What if he's a MONSTER in disguise?

What if I say hello to the monster and he pulls me down into his secret cave under the sand?

What if his cave is already full of other children, whose parents had told them the same thing – "Go and play with that little boy!"

I don't think Mum would be happy if I disappeared under the sand forever and went to live with the monster in his huge underground home.

The cave would be full of lost children like me.
We'd have to look after his pet moles,
and clean his floor, and comb his fur,
and cook his horrible, slimy dinner.

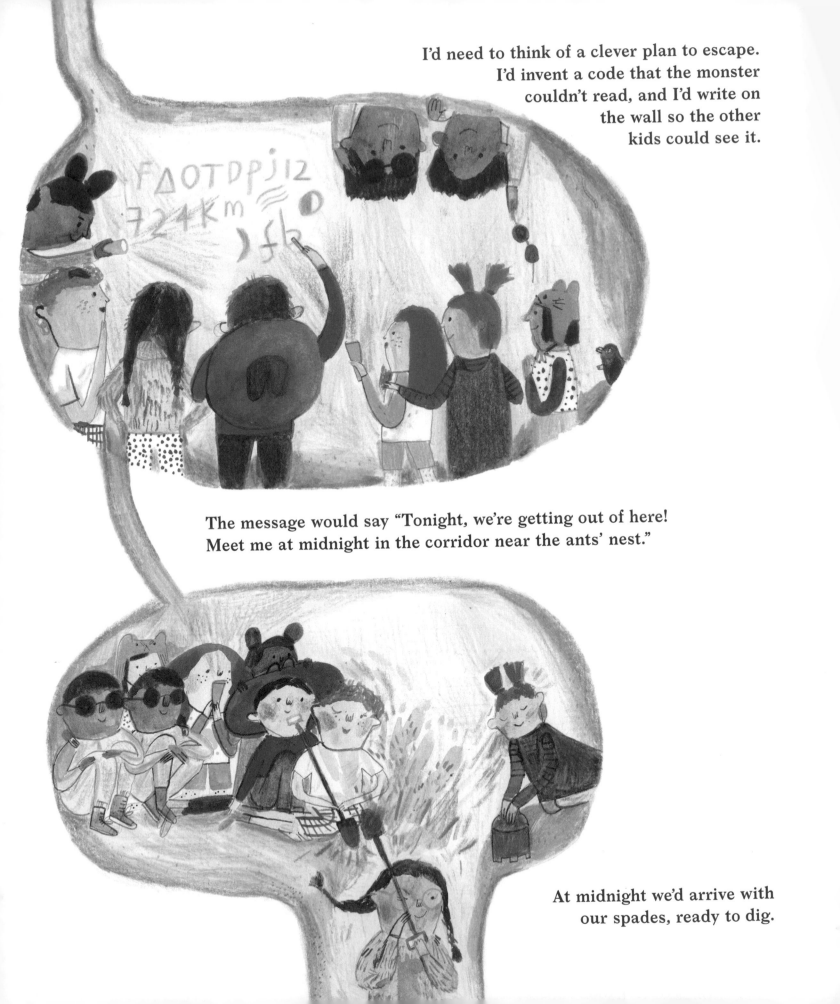

I'd need to think of a clever plan to escape. I'd invent a code that the monster couldn't read, and I'd write on the wall so the other kids could see it.

The message would say "Tonight, we're getting out of here! Meet me at midnight in the corridor near the ants' nest."

At midnight we'd arrive with our spades, ready to dig.

Eddie and Lily, the two strongest kids, would dig
a hole as big as a bear, and we'd follow behind.
But just as we were getting near the surface, the
monster would wake up with a growl...

...and we'd race to get out of the tunnel alive!

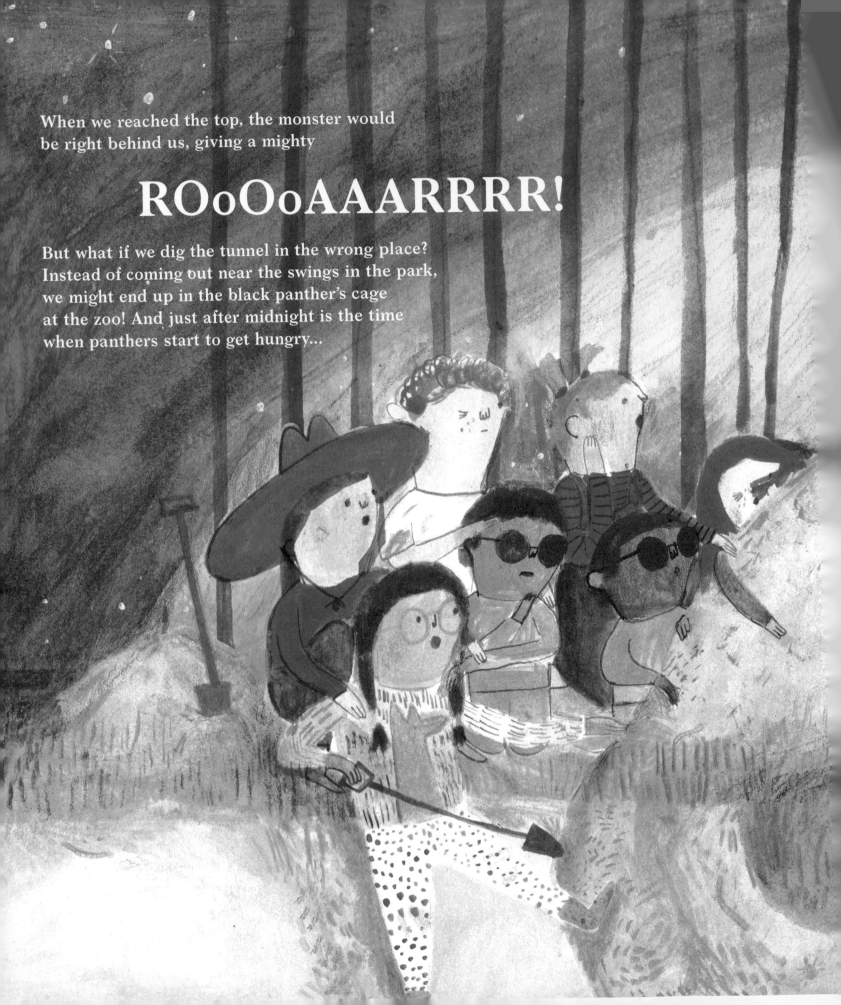

When we reached the top, the monster would
be right behind us, giving a mighty

ROoOoAAARRRR!

But what if we dig the tunnel in the wrong place?
Instead of coming out near the swings in the park,
we might end up in the black panther's cage
at the zoo! And just after midnight is the time
when panthers start to get hungry...

Things could get a bit dangerous. But luckily for us, the panther doesn't like the taste of humans and her favourite food is actually FRESH MONSTER MEAT.

So we'd hide in the corner of the cage and
the panther would wait for the monster to jump
out of the tunnel. It wouldn't be a pretty sight,
but we'd peek between our fingers if we dared.

After the panther had finished her huge dinner, she'd spend all night telling us stories about the jungle. We'd feel sorry for her, being locked up in a zoo. It's no life for a wild animal.

So we'd help her to get out of the cage
and find the railway station, where
she could take the first train
back to her homeland.

Then we'd wander through the streets in the early morning.
We'd buy fresh bread rolls to eat and climb up on the
rooftops to play with the cats and watch the sun rise.

When we got home, our parents would be so happy to see us.
We'd yawn and say "We're much too tired to go to school today!"

They'd feel bad because it was their fault that the monster had kidnapped us in the first place. So they'd let us stay at home and eat cakes all day.

And more importantly, they'd have learned their lesson. They'd never say "Go and play with that little boy!" ever again. We'd be allowed to play on our own if we wanted.